Dan, the Flying Man

W9-ATR-181

by Joy Cowley

FRANKLIN PIERCE
COLLEGE LIBRARY
RINDGE, N.H. 03461

I am Dan,
the flying man.

Catch me,
catch me
if you can.

Over a house

and over a crane.

Over a bridge

and over a train.

Over flowers,

8

over trees,

over mountains,

over seas.

I am Dan,
the flying man.

Catch me,
catch me
if you can.

All the people

ran and ran.

They caught Dan,
the flying man.